Snakes

Therese Shea

New York

Published in 2007 by The Rosen Publishing Group, Inc.
29 East 21st Street, New York, NY 10010

Book Design: Michael J. Flynn

Photo Credits: Cover © Lynsey Allan/Shutterstock; p. 5 © Anthony Bannister, Gallo Images/Corbis; pp. 7, 17 © Zig Leszezynski/Animals Animals; p. 9 (top) © Anna Lafrentz/Shutterstock; p. 9 (bottom) © Michael Lynch; p. 11 © Casey K. Bishop/Shutterstock; p. 13 © Alfred Wekelo/Shutterstock; p. 13 (inset) © Scott Pehrson/Shutterstock; p. 15 © SF Photography/Shutterstock; p. 19 © Noah Strycker/Shutterstock; p. 19 (inset) © Joe McDonald/Animals Animals; p. 21 (top) © Mircea Maieru/Shutterstock; p. 21 (bottom) © Doug Wechsler; p. 22 © Michael Ledray/Shutterstock.

Library of Congress Cataloging-in-Publication Data

Shea, Therese.
Snakes / Therese Shea.
p. cm. -- (Big bad biters)
Includes bibliographical references and index.
ISBN-13: 978-1-4042-3520-5
ISBN-10: 1-4042-3520-5 (library binding : alk. paper)
1. Snakes--Juvenile literature. I. Title. II. Series: Shea, Therese. Big bad biters.
QL666.O6S3984 2007
597.96--dc22
2006014646

Manufactured in the United States of America

Contents

Snakes with Legs?

Did you know that a long time ago there were no snakes? Many people think that some kinds of lizards used to hide in the ground. Their bodies slowly became long and legless. Finally, the lizards became the animals we call snakes!

Snakes can look scary. Some have long, thick bodies. Some make a rattling sound. Some have curved, **poisonous** teeth. Most snakes don't hurt people. In fact, they help people! Let's learn more facts about snakes!

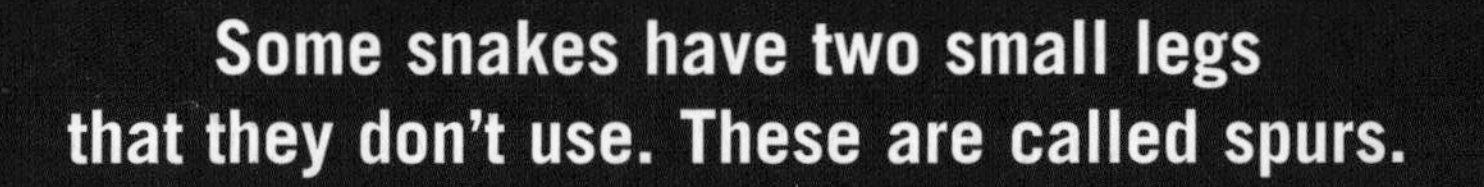

Some snakes have two small legs that they don't use. These are called spurs.

Skin and Scales

All snakes are covered with dry **scales**. Snakes even have clear scales over their eyes. This is why snakes don't blink or have eyelids. The color of their scales helps snakes hide. Green snakes can hide from enemies in grass. Brown snakes can hide in dirt.

Snakes never stop growing. As they grow and need more room in their skin, they crawl out of their old skin! This is called **molting**.

A snake may molt its skin several times a year.

Keeping Cool, Keeping Warm

People are **mammals**. Mammals are warm-blooded animals. This means the **temperature** in our bodies stays the same. Our surroundings do not control our body temperature.

Snakes are **reptiles**. Reptiles are cold-blooded animals. The outside world controls their body temperature. When they get too cold, they lie in the sun to warm up. When they get too warm, they lie in the shade to cool down.

These snakes are using their surroundings to warm up (top) and cool down (bottom).

A Tongue That Smells

Snakes have one eye on each side of their head. However, they cannot see well. They have ears on the inside of their heads but no openings on the outside. This makes it hard for snakes to hear well.

So how do snakes find food? How do they stay away from danger? You may have seen snakes sticking their tongues out. When they do this, they are "smelling" the air. The smells tell them if food or danger is near.

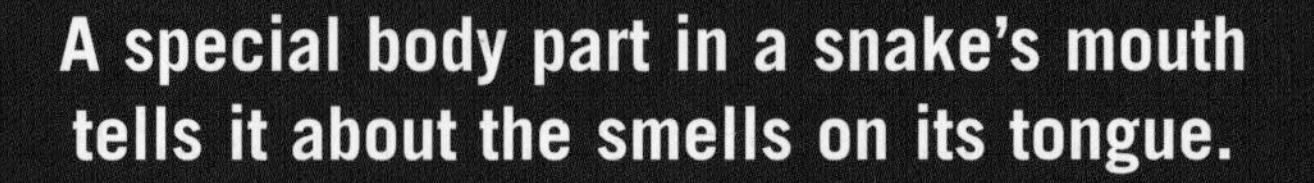

A special body part in a snake's mouth tells it about the smells on its tongue.

A Very Bad Bite

There are about 2,700 different kinds of snakes. All snakes have curved teeth. They use their teeth to hold their **prey** before swallowing it.

Some snakes have special teeth called **fangs** that hold a poison called **venom**. When these snakes bite, the venom will either kill the prey or make it unable to move. Then the snake can swallow the animal whole.

The boa that this girl is holding has teeth, but not fangs like the rattlesnake in the small picture.

A Big Meal

Snakes have bodies that help them swallow animals bigger than their heads. Their teeth hold the animal. They have jaws that stretch widely up, down, and sideways. Even their stomachs stretch! Sometimes snakes take an hour to swallow an animal.

Snakes do not have to eat very often. Snakes in zoos usually eat every few weeks. Sometimes a big snake in the wild can go for a year or more without eating!

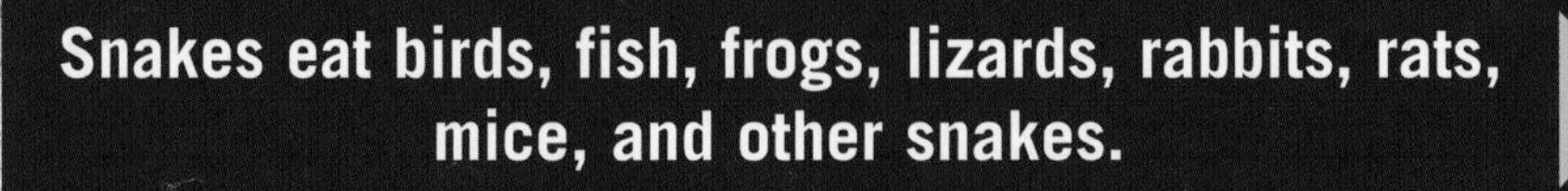
Snakes eat birds, fish, frogs, lizards, rabbits, rats, mice, and other snakes.

Garter Snakes

Garter snakes are common in North America. Most have three long stripes on their backs. They are usually about 18 inches (45.7 cm) to 50 inches (127 cm) long. You may have seen a garter snake where you live!

Garter snakes eat worms, fish, frogs, and mice. They catch them with their teeth. They do not have venom in their teeth. However, they have venom in their spit that slows down their prey. Their bite doesn't usually hurt people.

During the winter, many garter snakes like these may stay together in a cave to keep warm.

Pit Vipers

Pit vipers can be found in North and South America and in Southeast Asia. They have a special body part below each eye called a pit. The pits sense the body heat of prey. A pit viper can tell exactly where an animal is located—even in the dark!

Pit vipers have long fangs at the front of their top jaws. Some viper fangs are 2 inches (5.1 cm) long! The pit viper uses them to bite prey. Venom from the fangs enters the animal's body and kills it.

Rattlesnakes and copperheads are pit vipers. They have fangs like the one dripping venom shown here.

Pythons

Pythons live in Africa, Asia, and Australia. They have long, thick bodies. Most pythons grow to be about 16 feet (4.9 m) long. One python was over 33 feet (10.1 m) long!

Pythons also have pits to sense their prey. However, they don't have fangs with venom. Instead, they use their many curved teeth to hold their prey. Then they wrap their body around their prey and squeeze until the prey can't breathe. Large pythons can eat pigs, deer, antelope, and leopards.

A python can have over 100 teeth!

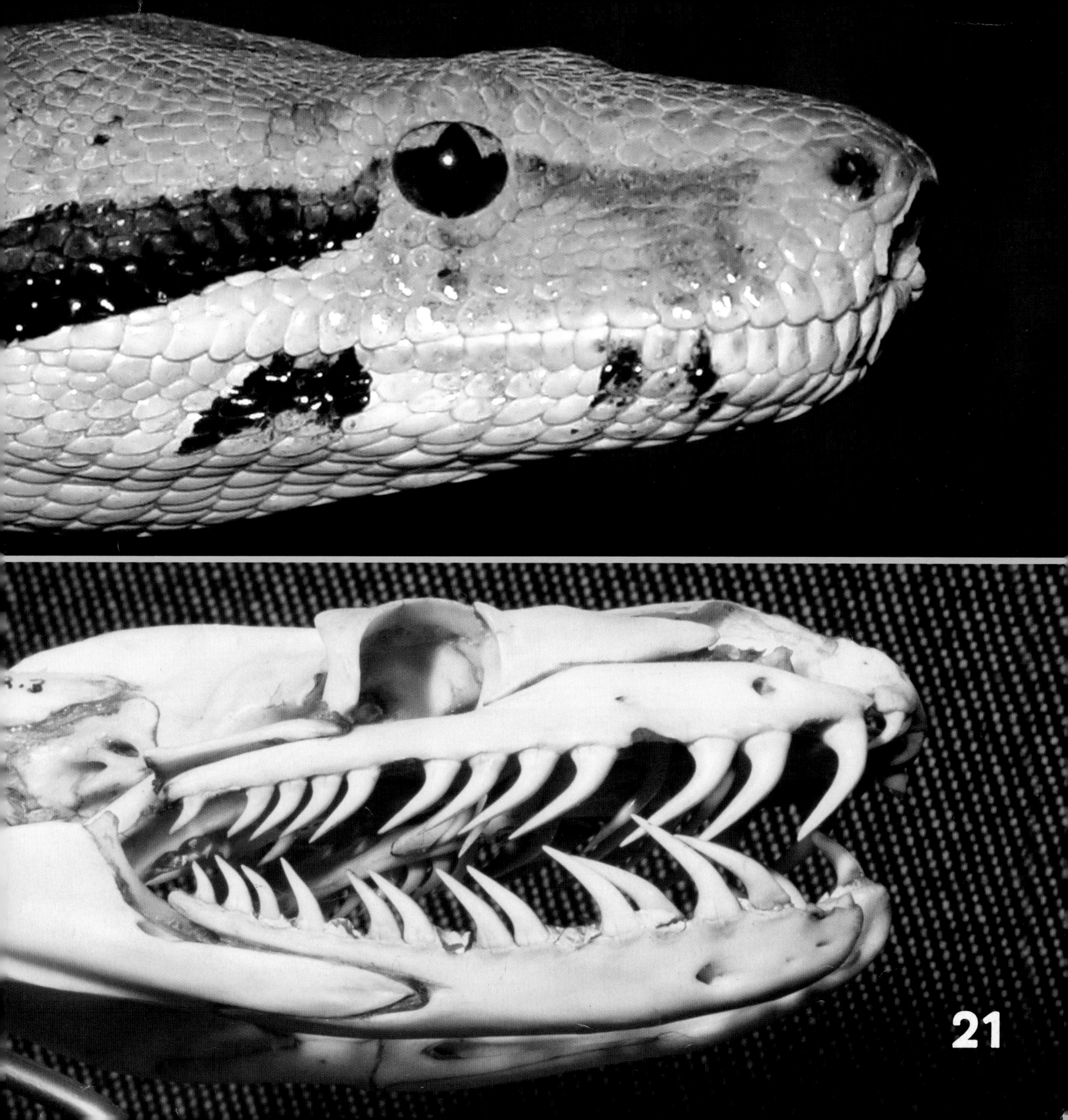

How Snakes Help

Snakes help people in many ways. They eat mice and rats that eat farm crops. Some doctors use venom to make **medicine**. Snakes are also food for many other animals. Snakes are an important part of nature and our world.

Remember, a snake that can hurt you can look like a snake that is harmless. It is a good idea to leave all snakes alone. All snakes will bite to guard themselves from danger.

Glossary

fang (FANG) A long, sharp tooth that a snake uses to put venom into an animal.

mammal (MAA-muhl) An animal that is often covered with hair or fur. Females give birth to live young and feed them milk from their bodies.

medicine (MEH-duh-suhn) A drug used to prevent or treat a sickness.

molting (MOHLT-ing) Shedding skin, fur, or other outer covering.

poisonous (POY-zuhn-uhs) Something that contains poison.

prey (PRAY) An animal that is hunted by another animal as food.

reptile (REHP-tyl) An animal that is usually covered with scales, like a snake or a lizard. A reptile is as warm or as cold as the air around it.

scale (SKAYL) A small plate that covers the bodies of some animals, such as snakes and fish.

temperature (TEHM-puhr-chur) How hot or cold something is.

venom (VEH-nuhm) Poison made by some snakes and other animals.

Index

Web Sites

Due to the changing nature of Internet links, PowerKids Press has developed an online list of Web sites related to the subject of this book. This site is updated regularly. Please use this link to access the list:
http://www.powerkidslinks.com/biters/snakes/